Alexandra Wallner

Since 1920

A Doubleday Book for Young Readers

A Doubleday Book for Young Readers
PUBLISHED BY DELACORTE PRESS
Bantam Doubleday Dell Publishing Group, Inc.
666 Fifth Avenue, New York, New York 10103
DOUBLEDAY and the portrayal of an anchor with a dolphin are
trademarks of Bantam Doubleday Dell Publishing Group, Inc.
Copyright © 1992 by Alexandra Wallner

Library of Congress Cataloging-in-Publication Data
Wallner, Alexandra.
Since 1920/by Alexandra Wallner.—1st ed.
p.   cm.
Summary: As the years pass a quiet country house is overtaken by
the growing city, until the granddaughter of the original homeowner
helps to restore the neighborhood to its former beauty.
[1. Dwellings—Fiction. 2. Cities and towns—Fiction.]
I. Title.
PZ7.W15938Si   1992
[E]—dc20   90-3646   CIP   AC
ISBN 0-385-41216-9
RL: 2.6

Typography by Lynn Braswell

All Rights Reserved

Printed in U.S.A.

September 1992

10 9 8 7 6 5 4 3 2 1

For my parents with love
—A.C.W.

In 1920, Mr. and Mrs. Walsh lived in a crowded, noisy city. But they wanted a quiet country home. So Mr. Walsh bought a piece of land from a farmer and built one.

Every day when Mr. Walsh was working, Mrs. Walsh brought him lunch in a basket.

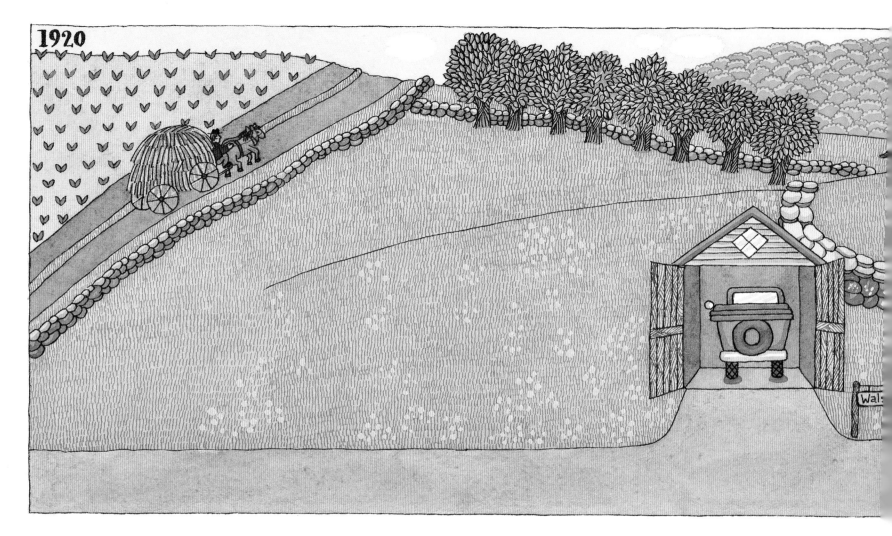

Mr. and Mrs. Walsh moved in that spring with their son, Stephan, who was three years old.

It was a cozy little house. The water for washing was outside and so was the bathroom. At night, oil lamps were used for light.

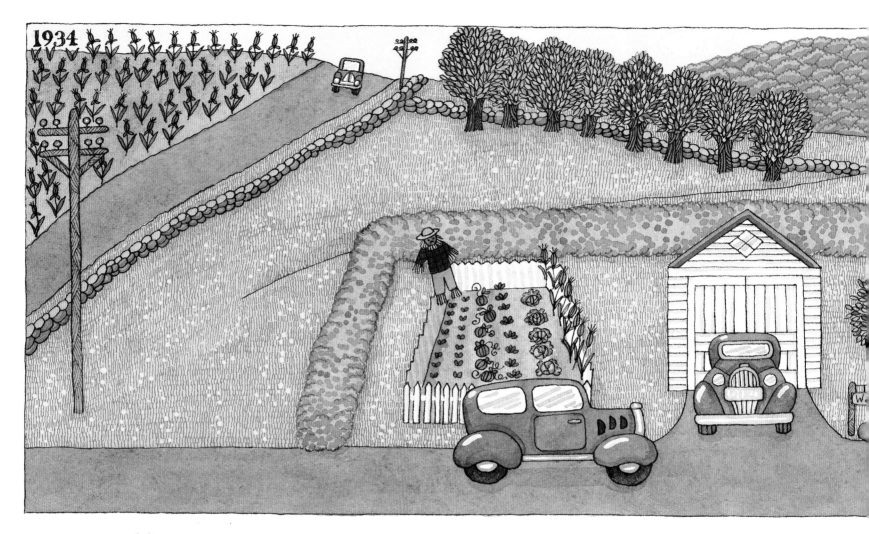

The years passed quietly in the cozy little house in the country. Not much changed. A new neighbor settled in a house beyond the cow pasture. A few more cars traveled the dirt roads.

The houses now had electricity and running water inside.

On the Fourth of July, neighbors and friends got together to have a picnic and tell stories.

One day, Mr. Walsh sold the part of his land that the garage was on to Mrs. Houser, a widow. She was going to live there with her daughter, Minnie, and make pies, cakes, cookies, and doughnuts to sell.

Minnie and Stephan, who was grown up now, liked each other very much right away.

The farmer who lived behind the Walshes' house grew old and retired. He sold much of his land.

In the winter of 1942 there was a big war in Europe. Stephan was a soldier and went there to fight. Everyone was very sad to see him go. Minnie was saddest.

The neighborhood did not change except that the blacksmith shop became an auto repair garage.

Mrs. Walsh and Mrs. Houser and a lot of other people grew their own fruits and vegetables during the war.

One day, when he came back from the war, Stephan married Minnie.

That spring, another young man who had been a soldier built a house in back of the Walshes'.

Other young men came back from the war, too, and built houses in the neighborhood.

Mrs. Houser's store grew. She started selling fresh foods as well as bakery goods. A new highway was built and more cars were on the road.

In the city beyond the hills where the Walshes had lived, people were building skyscrapers for offices and apartments. The city was getting bigger.

Minnie and Stephan built a house next door, where the Walshes' garden had been. Soon, their daughter, Hildy, was born.

More and more people moved into the neighborhood. More trucks, buses, and cars crowded the streets. It was almost as noisy as the city.

Mrs. Houser's store got bigger.

But it was too busy for Mr. and Mrs. Walsh. So they sold their house and moved to a small, quiet place by the ocean. Minnie, Stephan, and Hildy were very sad to see them leave.

Christmas became a busy time in the neighborhood. Almost all the
houses were now stores, where people came to shop for presents.

The city stretched right to the neighborhood street.

A few years later Mrs. Houser died. Her store became run-down.
The other stores in the neighborhood became run-down too. The cozy
little house where Mr. and Mrs. Walsh had lived was now a junk store.

The sidewalks became littered with trash. It was hard to keep up a house in a neighborhood where it seemed that nobody cared. So Minnie, Stephan, and Hildy sold their house and moved to the country, where it was clean and quiet.

One night a store caught fire. Soon the other stores and houses were burning too.

Firefighters worked all night, but…

...there was much damage.

For a long time the damaged buildings stood boarded up and abandoned.

Years passed. More and more people lived in the city and they needed houses. People took an interest in the old neighborhood again. They liked the charming way the old houses had been built. They wanted to clean and repair them to look like new.

Hildy, who was grown up now, bought the house her grandparents had built. She loved the little shuttered windows, the zigzaggy attic, and the snug porch where her grandparents used to sit. She fixed the house until it looked clean and friendly again.

People worked very hard to clean up the neighborhood. They built a park with benches and planted flowers and trees so that everyone could enjoy sitting outside in the city. They even built a playground for children.

The neighborhood was a nice place to live again.

Hildy was very happy living with her own family in the cozy little house that her grandparents had built in 1920.

Alexandra Wallner and her husband, John, live in a house in the Catskill mountains of New York that was built long before 1920.

"It had been a farmhouse once," the author says. "There was a large barn in the back which had caved in long ago and several small sheds.

"We loved the charm of it—the paned windows, low ceilings, the outdoor water pump, and the moss-covered stone walls."

On researching the history of the house, the author found that it had been built in 1825, and was once part of a very large farm stretching for many acres along the side of the mountain.

"Several parts of the house had been added over the years so it was a mixture of styles. The land around it had long been chopped up and divided and several houses stood around it."

Like Hildy in this story, the Wallners loved the pretty style of the old house and wanted to save it. "We cleaned it and fixed it and now it is nice to live in again."